THE GRAY ZONE

This special signed edition is limited to:

250 numbered paperback copies
26 lettered hardcover copies

This is copy __6__

John R. Little

THE GRAY ZONE

John R. Little
THE GRAY ZONE

ANAHEIM - CALIFORNIA

FIRST EDITION

The Gray Zone
© 2009 by John R. Little

Artwork © 2009 by Alan M. Clark
Foreword © 2009 by James A. Moore
Afterword © 2009 by John R. Little

This book is a work of fiction. Names, characters, places and incidents are either a product of the author's imagination or are used fictitiously. Any resemblance to actual events, locales or persons, living or dead, is entirely coincidental.

Cover Design, Interior Design & Typesetting
by César Puch

Copy Editing
by Jamie La Chance, Leigh Haig and Liz Scott

Bad Moon Books Logo Created by Matthew JLD Rice

BAD MOON BOOKS
1854 W. Chateau Ave.
Anaheim CA 92804
USA

www.badmoonbooks.com

*To my four wonderful sisters,
who have each given me much happiness
in their own ways:*

*Bonnie Harris
Wendy Waldie
Susan van Aarsen
Debbie Pfeiffer*

Foreword

Have you read John Little before? If yes, all the better. If no, welcome to a special place. But that's not why we're at this spot is it? We're here to discuss not the writer so much as the tome in your hands. *The Gray Zone.*

Oh, screw it. I wanna write about the writer first.

John Little is a treat. His voice and style are first class and I seriously have trouble understanding why he hasn't had a dozen novels out on best seller lists across the country. Seriously. It doesn't make a damned bit of sense. Judging by the level of talent he displays in everything of his I've read—which is not as much as I am hoping to read over the course of my lifetime, believe me—Little should be outselling at least half of the writers I've chosen to enjoy. Believe me, I've chosen to read one hell of a lot of writers over the years, so that's saying something. His writing is clean and crisp and delicious. No, I'm not trying to make you think of food, but there it is. His writing is like sinking your teeth into a favorite: tastes good every time.

As I've said before—and others have said before me—there seem to be two types of writers: Storytellers and Wordsmiths. One tells a story and the other crafts sentences that are damned near poetry by themselves. A few, a very few, really, seem capable of doing both with ease. John Little is one of those rarities. Oh, let's not misunderstand each other. I have no doubt in my mind that he works very hard at the job of telling stories, but he makes it look effortless. I respect that more than I can properly express, because I know how much of a challenge it can be. I love writing at least as much as I love reading, but I also know that some days the words don't want to come and other days they rush out in a disastrous mess. None of that shows up in Little's writing, though. If he succumbs to the challenges that face most writers, he hides them with the skill of a master artisan.

Enough of that. Have I mentioned that this is a time travel story? It is. You'd think, if you've been reading Little for a while, that he'd be done with those. He's not. I for one am grateful. Time travel stories are a bear. You do them the wrong way and nothing makes sense anymore. There's a good deal of fact checking in the average novel, but with time travel stories you have to check facts and then double check them, because it's easy to miss something crucial, some little detail that will make a few of the more attentive readers lose their place and cry foul. It happens with fair regularity. The thing is, once again, that if Little did make such a mistake (and I'm not saying he did), you don't give a good damn by the time it's all said and done. Because the story, the evolution of the characters, is so damned good that almost nothing is going to draw attention away from it.

Now, see, this is a foreword. That means I can't go on and on about the details of the story. That's okay. Even if I could, I wouldn't. I don't want to spoil the surprises. I will say this, however. I loved the ending. And I hated the ending. It was perfect and I wanted so damned much more. I really, truly think that's a gift. Little knows exactly where the story should end, exactly how to finish it. That isn't talent. That isn't artistry. That's a, pardon my French as the old saying goes, fucking miracle. It's easy to stop too soon and far, far too easy to ramble on for a long while, trying to find the right way to wrap everything up. John Little has managed to avoid the pitfalls of ending a tale on every occasion so far. That alone should win him the admiration of the masses. There are a few names much larger than mine that could take lessons from Little on that, believe me. Hell, I know he could teach me a thing or two.

Back to the main reason for this discourse, the story at hand. Yeah, I'm not telling you a damned thing. I won't let any of the secrets out and I won't reveal hint number one about the ending, except this: don't bother skipping forward to read the last page if you're one of that particular sad lot of readers. It won't do the least bit of good if you do. The ending won't make a lick of sense until you've read the rest.

Kick back, relax and get lost in the story that starts a few pages from here. The style is smooth and languid and the words are pure, sweet poetry. And when you're done, think about what I said and wonder for yourself exactly why the hell John Little isn't being read by a lot more people. For now he's like a little secret. I hope that doesn't last. Some secrets were never meant to be kept.

James A. Moore
May 30th, 2009
Marietta, Georgia

Chapter 1
Aswan (1984)

It's peaceful here. Has been all summer.

I didn't plan on staying in Egypt this long, but when I hopped onto the cruise ship going down the Nile in July, the idea of leaving seemed to fall away. Even though Cassie's waiting for me back in Montreal, the thrill of the ancient land asked me to stay

(just a little bit longer)

until now. The Egyptians have been so kind to me for the past three months, it's hard to imagine going back to the western world.

My home in Aswan is the back of a mud house. It was built by my landlord, Mohammed, who is only forty or fifty years old but looks seventy. He has a long gray beard and pencil-thin arms. He's weak and his eyes are runny and constantly leak.

Mohammed invited me to stay at the back of his home in exchange for teaching his son, Achmed, a bit of English. The deal was very one-sided, since Achmed already knows the language pretty well. Mostly we talk about how he likes Egypt and how it's different from Canada. He has trouble imagining so many things. Achmed is only thirteen years old, lively, always running around playing soccer in the streets with his friends, laughing and dancing as if the world is at his fingertips.

He's out in the street now, hopping to some internal rhythm, daring the neighbor boys to sneak a goal past him.

Achmed will almost certainly follow in his father's footsteps and grow old before his time. He's never seen a television set, could never imagine sitting in a comfortable easy chair watching Dallas or MASH or Johnny Carson. I'm not even sure there's a single TV set anywhere in the city. Maybe in the hotels.

Sometimes I hear music drifting out of houses or storefronts. Radios, tape recordings, maybe even some kids singing in a back room. The Egyptians love their music as much as we love *All in the Family*.

Achmed kicks his left leg out and makes an improbable stop. He's really on his game today.

"Great save!" I call to him.

He turns his head and takes a deep bow in mock appreciation. The other boys mutter and walk back toward their end of the makeshift soccer field. The ball is held together with brown tape, and it doesn't roll right, so it takes Achmed even more than a normal amount of concentration to shepherd it back down the street.

Back in Anjou, when I was his age, we played street hockey every winter. I always pretended to be Henri Richard, *The Pocket Rocket*, my favorite player from the Montreal Canadians. Anjou is a suburb of Montreal, and everybody there is hockey crazy. Sometimes even the adults played street hockey with us.

I shared the same name as my hero. Well, almost. Henry, not Henri, since my parents were English. I always hated that "y" at the end of my name. When my mom wasn't around, I always pronounced my name Henri, with a flamboyant French accent. *Ahn-RHEE!*

Here in Aswan, everyone plays soccer instead of hockey, but I can live inside Achmed's mind and understand the intensity he plays the game with. He kicks and has his shot blocked by his friends. The ball bounces over and hits a small dust-covered car. I've never asked Achmed who his favorite player is. I'll have to do that. Not that the name will mean anything to me—all the games are broadcast only in Arabic.

"He good."

I turn and smile at Mohammed, who's watching his son hop backward down the dirt road that passes for the main street here.

I nod. "He's having fun, don't you think? The freedom of the young, right?"

I'm not sure if Mohammed understands every word I say. Likely not. He's glancing sideways at me as if he's unsure whether I've really asked him a question or not. He finally nods his head slightly.

"Felucca ride to south islands. Tomorrow. You come?"

I hesitate, wanting to be sure I heard him right through his thick accent.

I've never been invited onto Mohammed's felucca before. I think it's an honor thing. Something about only family and close friends being allowed in the boat. Hell, I don't really know what the deal is, but I know it's a big thing to him that he asked me to join.

"Sure. I'd love to. What time?" I point to my watch. Mohammed's always been fascinated by my Timex, especially the silver-colored chain. I see his eyes arrow right onto the watch face, squinting to look at the hands. When I leave Aswan next week, I'm going to give it to him as a farewell gift. I'm not sure what he'll do when the battery runs out, but it should last him a while.

"Sunrise. Bring water."

Mohammed and his family will just scoop water to drink from the Nile, but I can't do that without getting sick.

"Achmed steer felucca. First time."

I bow my head to Mohammed. "Very kind of you to invite me."

Without saying anything else, he shuffles back inside his house. There's no door and the only windows are empty holes between the mud bricks. The walls are stronger than they look. I've seen Achmed bounce his soccer ball off the walls for an hour without the slightest dent showing.

Achmed has the ball again and is trying to keep it in the air with his feet. It looks like an overgrown hacky-sack. He's been like a son to me. Well, maybe not *exactly* like a son. I mean, I'm only twenty-two myself, and he's thirteen, so maybe he's more like a little brother. Whatever, he basically adopted me when I first landed in Aswan. My first stop of course was the High Dam. It's one of the biggest tourist attractions in the city, so of course I went there.

Big mother of a dam, let me tell you.

And standing in the middle, near the concession stand, was Achmed. He ran from one side of the dam to the other, looking out at the huge expanse of Lake Nasser on one side, running fifty feet to the other side to see the comparatively small trickle of water that eventually flowed to Cairo and beyond.

"Baksheesh!" he'd shout to every tourist.

At first I waved him off. All kids in Egypt call for baksheesh to every tourist they see. They know we almost never give any money, but they figure what have they got to lose by asking?

Achmed was different from the others. He came right up to me, beamed a smile with his entire face, and just grabbed my attention like no other kid ever had before. He wore an off-white galabea, the same as all the other boys. I could see it was a size or two too small, but that didn't seem to bother him. Once I stared into his eyes, it was impossible not to give him a few piastres.

"Thank you, sir," he said with a formal bow.

I laughed at the scene, feeling like I was an actor in a Shakespearean comedy.

"You speak English."

"Some. Not good like you, sir."

And he bowed again, laughed, and pocketed the change as he turned to look for other tourists.

"Hey, do you know the city good enough to be a tour guide?"

Achmed was caught a bit off guard. I doubt he'd been asked that before.

"Some. I can take to big market and quarry. Big obelisk there." He paused to think. "Maybe Papa take to Elephantine Island. Maybe Philea. Cleopatra's bathtub there. Bring rubber duck for picture."

So began our three months together.

It's hard to think about leaving. I've told Mohammed it's time for me to go home, and I'm pretty sure that's why he arranged for me to go with the family on their felucca tomorrow. I'm also convinced it's why it's going to be Achmed's first time to steer. To say good-bye to me.

I haven't told Achmed I'm leaving yet. After the ride. I've still got to figure out how to get back to Cairo and arrange a flight back. Maybe Cassie can arrange the trip. Probably easier for her than me. The phones in Aswan are very unreliable, and finding a travel agent who can actually book a flight from Cairo to Canada would be a challenge.

Achmed's game is breaking up. The ball belongs to one of the other players who's carrying it off. I'll buy a new ball for Achmed as a farewell gift.

It's late afternoon. Time for a nap. I yawn and tussle Achmed's curly black hair as we walk into his home.

The house is really just one big room, with a few large cubby-holes for bedrooms. The walls are made of uneven dry mud, covered with brightly-colored portraits to disguise the roughness of the surfaces. The pictures are caricatures of long-dead relatives. I think the two largest are Mohammed's mother and father. They look even older then he does, but of course who knows? Everyone looks old here. The heat, the hard work, the lack of food . . . it all combines together to rip the years off the local citizens.

Achmed sits in a corner on a small mat. Soon, he'll lay down and sleep there.

The main part of the house only has a small table with benches on each side. A stone oven is built into one wall. Two gray pigeons sit on a small ledge, quietly looking around the room. They don't know that one day they'll end up inside the oven.

On the other side of the room is a small terrarium, with wire mesh reaching up about six inches on all sides. I pick up one of the baby crocodiles and hold it in my hand. The other two crocs ignore me. It still seems weird to have crocodiles as pets. The one I'm holding sits and looks at me without fear; it's smaller than my index finger. I put it back alongside the others, near the water inside the cage.

I walk through the center of the house and out the far side. There's no back yard or anything, just a small area of debris. I've got a small pile of hay I sleep on. Beggars can't be choosers, and the one thing I wanted to do on my trip was to see what real Egyptians live like. I'm not sure everyone lives like this, but this is certainly one way. I lie down and close my eyes, thinking of Cassie.

I wake just as the sun is starting to lighten the sky. My neck is sometimes sore after sleeping on the hay, but today, it's not too bad. It's near the end of August, and it's already eighty degrees out. A good day to spend on the water.

Achmed is near the door, not far from me. He's kneeling on his small rug, facing south. I just watch and keep quiet. After a few moments of prayer, he rolls up his mat and walks into the house. Only after he places his rug back in storage does he come back out and smile at me.

"We ride Nile today."

I nod. "And you'll be steering. Are you nervous?"

Achmed lowers his head a bit, but I can see he's dying to shout to all his friends about the big day. "Papa has big felucca. Nobody steers but him before."

"Achmed!"

The yell comes from inside the house. It's his mother. Instantly, Achmed jumps to attention and walks inside.

I barely know Shani. She's never spoken to me, and I have no idea if she knows a word of English. She wears dark purple or green robes that cover her head, but unlike the most devout women in the city, she lets her face show. Her eyes are brown and sad.

Mohammed's other two wives are nowhere in sight.

Achmed is almost as tall as Shani, so she faces him and whispers a long set of instructions to her son. She's staring him right in the eyes, imploring him to listen, to be careful. I know she's likely telling him to be strong, be a warrior, don't disgrace your father.

In my mind, though, she's saying, "Hold on tight and don't let your feet slip. You know how easy it is to fall. Are your feet strong enough? You don't have to do this yet, you know. We can call it off. Maybe you're too young."

Just like a Canadian mother.

Achmed answers in reassuring tones and tells her he's going to be very careful, that his feet are agile and strong, and that he'll be back home before she even knows he's gone.

Or maybe she's telling him to get out and feed the chickens, and he's answering he'll do it when he gets home.

Just like a Canadian teenager.

Whatever the actual words, Shani sneaks a look over at me. She looks like she blames me for making her child grow up too fast. Then, she gives Achmed a quick hug. She walks out the front door and off to do whatever she has planned for the day.

"Where's your father?" I ask.

"To the dock. We go meet him."

Achmed's house is hidden in a small clump behind the Mena Hotel, about a ten minute walk from the Nile. The scattered houses look like they were built at random locations, sometimes only a few feet apart. I'd walked down there many times before, because in all of Egypt, the world revolves around the river. Without the Nile, there would be no Egypt. It's just as true now as in Biblical times.

More than 200,000 people live in Aswan, but it still manages to have the charm of a small town, where everybody knows everybody else.

I sometimes imagine Mohammed walking into a bar and having everyone yell out, "Norm!"

Except of course, there's no bars in Aswan. Or if there are, they're well-hidden, and I've never seen them. I've heard that rich Saudi sheiks know where to go to drink, gamble, and do other things they can't do at home, but those places are secreted from me.

Mohammed has the felucca all set. The sail is already raised, towering thirty feet above the hull. We walk on a wobbly narrow plank leading us onto the boat. Mohammed talks to Achmed in Arabic, and I again imagine a last minute chance to change his mind.

Achmed laughs and moves to the far end of the sailboat.

Mohammed pulls the plank in and unties the felucca, pushing us in a small arc onto the river.

Achmed climbs up and soon I can only see his feet. I know that hidden from view, he's using his hands to do something to control the sails. A half-inch thick rope hangs down, which I think is somehow connected to what he's doing above. His bare feet control the rudder, gently moving the control lever back and forth. I recognize some of the movements from when he was playing hacky-sack with the soccer ball.

"You're doing great, Achmed!" I call up to him. He doesn't answer, but I know he'll be beaming that huge smile of his.

We're sailing quite fast, and the wind feels good in my face. Mohammed sits and stares at Achmed's feet, while I sightsee.

I'd taken a felucca ride earlier in the summer. It's one of the must-do activities for tourists, and there's never a problem finding somebody to zip you around in their boat for a few Egyptian pounds.

Not Mohammed's, though. As near as I can tell, he inherited the boat from his father, and maybe it was passed down from earlier generations, too. To Mohammed, it's sacred.

My eyes close of their own volition. Cool breezes glance off my face, and all I can feel is happiness. I wish Cassie was with me, but I'll be home soon, and one day, I'll bring her back to show her where I spent my magical summer. Aswan just might be the best city in the world.

Ninety-three days I've been here. And I think every one of those days, a different stranger was kind to me. It's just the way of Egypt. What's not to love?

"We go Philea."

I blink my eyes open to see Mohammed looking at me.

"Cleopatra's bathtub?"

A tear leaks from his left eye. Even so, he smiles and nods. "Island moved when high dam built. Otherwise would drown."

"Like Abu Simbel?"

"Statues cut in pieces and put back together."

There are still a million things about Aswan I don't know. Sadness rushes over me as I realize I'm running out of time to discover everything. A renegade thought trips through my mind: Why do I have to go back to Canada?

And then the ever-present image of Cassie appears and answers that.

"Help!"

Mohammed and I both turn to the back of the felucca. I wonder why Achmed called out in English, but that thought is swallowed easily as I see no scrawny boy using his feet to steer.

Only the dangling rope hanging down. The boat is spinning in lazy circles now, and I grab onto the side. I also have to duck as the boom of the sails swing by.

"Achmed!" Mohammed is on his feet, years of practice allowing him to dance easily to the other end of the boat, where his son should be.

He calls out again, but there's no answer. I pull myself along the side of the swinging boat, looking out to the water.

There!

Behind us, already about forty feet away, I see Achmed's small head bouncing around. There's a red smear being washed away from his brow, but it reappears, and I know he's cut badly. He must have hit his head when he slipped. He isn't moving, just being bounced around by the waves.

Mohammed groans and covers his mouth. "Achmed!" He grabs the rudder, to turn the boat, but there's no way he can get there in time.

There's no time to think—instinct takes over, and I dive from the side of the boat. It's easier than trying to climb all the way to the back of the boat while it's rocking. The water is warm and clear. I swim as far as I can underwater and finally surface, taking in a huge breath.

Part of me remembers not to swallow the water, but mostly I just swim as fast as I can.

Achmed isn't there anymore.

I turn around and see the felucca well behind me. Mohammed is holding his arm straight out, pointing to my right. I follow his direction and swim farther, taking another look back.

How long has he been under water?

Mohammed points downward.

I dive; the water gets dark as soon as I'm under a few feet.

I can't see anything, but I wave my arms around, hoping to hit Achmed by accident.

Nothing.

I keep going deeper and deeper, feeling the pressure build up in my lungs, but I don't care. I can't leave him. Down farther.

That first day we met, Achmed told me, "Nile brings life to all of us."

(And takes it, too.)

No. Not today.

My lungs are burning, and I know I'll have no choice but to swim back to the surface soon. I start to panic, wondering if I can actually make it back or if I'll be drowning along with my little friend.

And then I hit something. It didn't really feel like a body, but I grab onto it and change direction, pulling myself and the thing I'm holding back up to the surface. Bubbles of air escape my mouth, and just for a second I lose my hold. Instinctively I grab the thing again and double my efforts. *I'm not going to make it.* I'm going to die and Cassie will never know what happened to me.

Suddenly, the water color lightens and then I'm above the surface. I gulp the wonderful air into my lungs, and at the same time, I pull the dead thing up.

It's a foot. I twist Achmed around and get his head above the water while I paddle. His eyes are closed. I breathe into his mouth and hit his chest, not really knowing what I'm doing, just that I have to try *something*.

And somehow I hit the right combination. He spits out water and gulps a deep breath, coughing and spitting, his eyes bulging in terror.

The blood starts to flow again on his forehead, but that's the

least of our worries.

Mohammed has turned the felucca around and pulls up near us. I push Achmed's arm up and Mohammed grabs onto it, pulling him into the boat. I didn't think he had the strength to do that, but he does it without hesitation. Once he sees that Achmed is breathing okay, he helps me over the side, too.

I collapse and try to catch my breath.

Mohammed goes to a bench and lifts the seat, pulling out a first aid kit, or at least a reasonable facsimile. He's talking quietly to Achmed, but I don't understand anything he says. I don't think he's berating him. It looks like he's telling him how brave he was. Maybe that's just what I want to believe.

Achmed ends up with a cotton bandage around the top of his head. I hope he gets to see a doctor, but I know that's not very likely. He'll carry a bad scar on his forehead for the rest of his life.

I'm holding the stick that controls the rudder so we go more or less straight. There's not much of a wind right now, so the sail doesn't move. We're almost stationary while Mohammed takes care of Achmed. I feel like an outsider, a peeping Tom watching as the father kisses the son on the cheek and hugs him. He whispers and smiles, and Achmed eventually smiles back at him.

One day, I'd like a son.

With the excitement dying down, I free myself to think again of Cassie. She's waiting back in the McGill ghetto for me to come home, probably wondering why in God's name I could possibly want to stay so long in Egypt. I can hear her saying, "How many pyramids could you possibly look at?"

I smiled at the thought. She'd never really think that. Cassie's happy when I'm happy. I know that. When I tell her about my summer, I know the first words out of her mouth will be,

"You've *got* to take me there."

Mohammed leans back and smiles at Achmed. In English, and in a loud voice, he says, "Good first steer."

Achmed actually laughs, and I smile. Mohammed looks at me and raises his eyebrows.

"Terrific job!" I say. "You've really got a story to tell your friends now."

Mohammed comes over and sits beside me, unconsciously taking control of the rudder device.

"You save him." He puts his hand on my shoulder. "I thank you kind."

The look in his eyes tells me everything. He wouldn't have been able to swim out to save his son.

"I have gift."

"Oh, no," I say. "You don't need—"

"Yes. Please to steer."

I take the wooden arm from him as he prances cat-like to the front of the felucca. He moves some pieces of wood around and opens a small drawer hidden behind. When he comes back to me, he's carrying a small, purple velvet pouch.

"Ramesses the Great was king of time," he says. He's looking into my eyes, as if daring me to contradict him. I know about Ramses II, of course. He was the greatest of the ancient pharaohs. I had no idea what Mohammed means about the king of time, though. I assume it's an error in his English.

He pulls the drawstring on the pouch, and I see there are two small yellow vials inside.

"From my father. From his father." Mohammed seems to want to say more, back to more generations, but he doesn't have the words for that.

"Stole long ago from Ramesses tomb." He uses the Egyptian

name when he speaks, a softer version compared to the English *Ramses*.

"Really?" I must look like an idiot. The only tomb in recent history that was found with anything inside was King Tutankhamen. Either this is nonsense, or those vials are very, very old.

"Ramesses the king of time," he says again. "I save for Achmed. You take one."

He hands a vial to me and motions for me to open it. I twist the cap off and hear the snap of air rushing in. Inside is a dusting of white powder. Following Mohammed's pantomimes, I pour the powder into my left hand.

"Eat."

He reaches into the Nile and scoops some water into the palm of his hand. "Take water."

I don't know how to argue, how to tell him the Nile is full of micro-organisms that will likely make me sick if I drink it. He swallows the water in his palm.

What the hell. I'm going home. Who cares if I'm sick for awhile on the plane? And I can't insult my friend.

Besides, I know I already swallowed some water when I was searching for Achmed.

I follow his lead and scoop some water into my empty hand.

When I hesitate, he again says, "Eat." He points at the powder. "Time . . . " Again, he seems to want to say more, to explain, but the words fail him.

After three months of living with Mohammed, there's no question of trust. I swallow the gritty stuff. It immediately dissolves into a bitter liquid that sticks to my tongue. I almost choke, but Mohammed moves my hand to my mouth, and I swallow the clear Nile water. It's cool and tastes wonderful.

I scoop another handful of water, to wash away the last of the bitter taste.

"Time. You go to time now."

I nod, without any understanding at all.

Achmed is smiling at me. I wonder if he knows what the heck this is all about.

"Move now. I steer us home."

"I guess I'll never get to see the bathtub, eh?"

Mohammed smiles, showing his few remaining teeth. "Big hole. Doesn't look like bathtub."

"But it was Cleopatra's, right?"

He climbs up, and I move to sit by Achmed. Mohammed's feet take control of the steering mechanism as he controls the sails above. He grabs the dangling rope Achmed must have tripped on between two toes and moves it aside.

I put an arm around Achmed, and he leans in to me. I know Cassie would have some wise and kind words to say to him, to tell him how good he did, that next time he'd be way better. That it's not his fault, that steering a felucca is a hard trade, that he should be really proud.

I say none of those things. In truth, I don't know how hard it is to steer a felucca. I stay quiet, just hold Achmed to me, thinking more of Cassie than of him.

Cassie is amazing. Smart, pretty, and sexy. I think of the first time I saw her . . .

Chapter 2
Montreal (1982)

... huh?

Mohammed is . . . gone. Achmed, too.

My feet aren't lifting up and down of their own volition to counter the action of the Nile waves.

I'm looking out through my own eyes, but nothing makes any sense. My breathing is ragged and hard, and I find myself leaning over a bit, light-headed and

(scared)

confused. The things I'm seeing are coming from a place that can't be. Instead of the desert sun beating down on me with the cool breeze brushing my cheeks, the sky is now overcast, and a threat of a storm hangs in the air.

Gone are the other feluccas, the grimy sea scent, my own light blue galabea I always wear so I mix in with the Egyptians. Now, I'm wearing jeans and a tee shirt. I recognize the upside-down words on my chest, *Rolling Stones Tour*. It's from 1978.

I shake my head and take a deep breath. There's a lamp post

beside me I use to steady myself.

I must be going crazy. Or dreaming. A nightmare, more like it. But, I feel *real*. I know it's not a dream.

Hundreds of people are lined down the street, all staring at the passing parade. Far to my left, multi-colored floats grind their way down St. Catherines Street, and they stretch forever to my right as well.

St. Catherines?

Yes. I recognize it immediately, with the many stores huddled side by side with French signs advertising new records, books, souvenirs, and clothing.

I'm in Montreal.

And I also know *when* I am. It's the day I met Cassie.

There's a bagel store behind me, and the fresh smell of the dough drifts all around me. It's a scent I'll never forget. I lived in and around Montreal for twenty years, and the city etched itself into me like fingerprints.

"Salut!" A hockey player is sitting on the trunk of a convertible, his feet dangling into the back seat. He's waving and calling out. If I wasn't so confused, I'd know who he is, but right *now*, it's all an impossible blur running through my mind—like rerunning an old eight millimeter movie my father took of us when we played street hockey.

It's June 24th. *La Fete Nationale.* Quebec's national holiday. Up on the mountain, celebrations would be going on all day long. It's the first holiday of summertime, and the one all families look forward to. I can imagine little kids wading out into Beaver Lake, while their parents sit around the edges, talking and laughing with the strangers beside them.

I met Cassie at this parade. I followed her and—

Oh, my God. There she is.

The float is stopped right in front of me. Maybe farther down St. Cathy's, an earlier float had to slow down or stop due to some small hitch.

The Eniskillen Marching Accordion Band is right *here*. Twelve accordion players with two bass drummers at the rear, marching in place while playing "When Irish Eyes Are Smiling."

Some of the accordionists are off key, but they smile and laugh, and the crowd cheers them on. There's a little girl dancing an Irish jig near me.

Most of the musicians are about forty years old. The one in the middle of the last row is Cassie's father. He's fat and balding and is sweating, even though it's not a hot day.

My eyes leap to the front of the float. Two baton twirlers do their thing, tossing their rods into the air and making unlikely catches before they hit the ground. Although they're synchronized with each other, they aren't really in step with the accordions. Not that it matters.

The girl on the far side has long red hair, bright *fire* hair. She wears a perpetual smile I know isn't at all related to being on show. It's just the way she always is.

My heart is pounding, and again I feel a bit faint, clutching again at the lamp post for support. I must be

(dreaming)

dreaming. But, no. It's too real. I feel alive, living through this weird déjà vu thing exactly like it happened the first time.

Cassie has more people's attention than any of the accordion players. She's tall and thin and when she tosses her baton, it's with utmost confidence that it will come back to her fingers. She even glances at the audience at times while twirling behind her back.

She looks right at me.

I feel an amazing electric shock as we lock eyes. I'm sure her smile grew even larger when she saw me, but now she turns to look at the other side of the street.

She doesn't recognize me.

"Alors!" shouts the hockey player in the car ahead of the band, as they all start inching down St. Cathy's again.

I still don't understand. Just a few minutes ago, I was with Mohammed and Achmed. How'd I get to Montreal two years ago?

Part of me doesn't really care, and as I think about Achmed, I can no longer quite picture his face. I know he's got thick black curly hair and a big smile, but those are just words right now rather than real memories. The missing image of my little friend overpowers seeing Cassie just for a moment. I try to focus on Mohammed, with his scraggly gray beard and the mask of wrinkles he wears, but I can't quite get a clear image. I know I'll meet him in my future, and that memory is out there, but it's fading, the same as normal memories fade after not being used for a time.

Shit.

The marching band is far enough down the street that I can only hear the occasional bar of their music. Another band is coming closer and drowning out the accordions.

Cassie.

I can't see her.

A few drops of rain start to splash down as I maneuver my way through the crowd. Some people raise umbrellas, making it even harder to get through. Finally, I duck onto the road, beside a truck pulling a giant blue telephone from Bell Canada. It's covered in bright pink flowers and is flanked with a sign advertising their services. There's a man in a tuxedo on the float waving at the crowd. We all ignore him, since nobody knows who he is.

I walk briskly, and after about five minutes I catch up with the Eniskillen marching band. Cassie is still there, flinging her baton into the air, but the drizzle is making it harder for her to see. Doesn't matter; she never misses.

The parade turns north on Crescent Street and into the party district. We pass *The Wrong Number*, my favorite place to drink, along with *Thursdays* and all the other nightclubs and bars. Tonight, the street will be blocked off to traffic while thousands of people zip around, checking out all the pick-up spots.

The parade ends near the bottom of Mount Royal. There's a large parking lot behind the hospital, and here, all the attractions disband and pack up for the day. Most of the floats are folded in on themselves, and the place looks like a giant's playspace, where he's scattered a bunch of toys around in all directions.

The rain's stopped, at least temporarily, but Cassie's bright blue dress has darker circles spotting it. The pattern almost looks deliberate.

"You're awfully good with that baton," I say. I smile, but I'm nervous and can't quite seem to make it work.

"Thanks!" She pats the side of her outfit. "I'm a bit of a mess, though."

For a few seconds, I don't know what to say. Cassie looks at me expectantly.

"I'm Henry." Weird, I just introduced myself to the woman I've loved for the past two years. I did it without thinking, as if we've never met.

"Cassie. Cassie McDougall." She nods and then looks around. "That's my dad. He's driving me back home. Nice to meet you." She starts to walk off.

"Wait!"

She looks back at me. "Yes?"

And that smile hits me. Not her *normal* brilliant smile, but the special one. The one I sometimes think she reserves just for me. She leans slightly forward, staring deep into my eyes. I can see her tongue slightly lifting in her mouth, as if she's reaching out to kiss me.

And then the sun comes out, shining through the clouds, as if ordered by God himself to show this girl in the best possible light.

We both glance up and for some reason it seems extraordinarily funny. Both of us snicker. This is the moment I fall in love. My heart seems to skip a beat, and my throat tightens. I can't seem to breathe. All I can do is stare at her.

"Are you free? I mean for, like, dinner?" I finally ask.

"It's not even lunch time yet."

Stupid moron, I chide myself. "Well, lunch. That's what I meant."

"I don't go for meals with boys I've just met."

For a second, I'm not sure how to answer that. Of course she wouldn't go out with strangers. "You can invite your Dad."

Oh, shit, just what I'd like. First date with her father tagging along.

She brushes her red hair back past her shoulders and seems to consider. "Maybe just to someplace nearby. I'll tell Dad I'll meet him at home. Wait here."

Before she leaves, she leans in to me and asks, "You're not some kind of weirdo, are you?"

Before I can answer, she laughs and looks behind her.

As she talks to her father, the weirdness hits me again. It didn't strike me as odd when I talked to her except for that one thing about introducing myself; it was just like we were meeting for the first time. In fact, we spoke word for word exactly what I remember us saying two years ago.

Or just now.

What happens next? I wonder. Vague future memories swirl around my mind. We'll walk south, looking for a place to eat and will start talking. We'll both be surprised to see we end up all the way in Old Montreal. We pop in for pancakes. No, crepes.

The memories aren't clear; it's like trying to remember what I had for a specific meal a long time ago. But these are memories of my future.

While Cassie talks to her father, I wonder again what happened to Achmed. I wish I knew . . .

Chapter 3
Aswan (1984)

Achmed is patting his head, holding the towel into place as Mohammed steers the felucca back into his tiny dock.

What?

Now, I'm even more confused. I was just with Cassie. Wasn't I? She's talking to her father. I sit quietly on the boat, wondering if I'm going crazy. I can feel the gaze of her eyes on me, much stronger than all the memories of her I brought to Egypt. It was just a moment ago.

"I know," says Achmed, responding to something I must have said. "But maybe Papa stop letting me steer again."

Words come out of my mouth, even though I'm still fighting for context. "I'm sure you'll be back in the saddle again very soon. Probably as soon as your head heals."

"Stupid rope."

I'm kicking myself for not saying something about the rope when it dangled down onto the back end of the boat. Now I can see that Mohammed doesn't let it near his feet. I should have noticed the difference.

"You'll never make that mistake again."

Achmed looks out to the water and scoops up a drink. He knows I'm just saying platitudes, and that's not helping.

Soon, the boat nudges the dock, and we all climb out while Mohammed loops a rope around the tethering pole.

Achmed is light on his feet and easily hops out, walks right off toward the city. He wants to be alone.

The older man is slower, tying the sails down, checking that various locks are set, then allows me to help him to the dock. He doesn't need the hand, of course, but it's a gesture of friendship.

"Achmed's not happy," I say.

Mohammed nods. "Better tomorrow."

"Will you let him steer again?"

Mohammed looks me in the eyes like I was an idiot, and I know there's some other Egyptian tradition I'm not aware of.

"He master of felucca now. I help."

The summer heat is intense and debilitating. I hadn't noticed it much on the water, but now we're back, it's like we're baking inside his small stone oven at full heat. I feel my energy draining with every step.

"Tea."

I nod as Mohammed leads the way through a maze of streets to a small shop. There's only three tables in the place. No front door. Hell, no *front* at all. Same as most of the shops here. There's just the tables, sitting on the sidewalk with the owner working a bit farther back. Fortunately, there's a roof with a ceiling fan, so it's much cooler.

Mohammed chats with the owner for a few minutes, talking as much with his hands as with his mouth. I smile and nod when he looks or points toward me. I'm sure he's talking about the trip and how I rescued Achmed. I wish he'd hold the chatter till after the tea arrives.

Eventually, a young girl comes out with our tea on a plate. The owner yells at her. She nods and goes back to bring out a hookah pipe. It's a nice shiny one with apple chips mixed in to add a fruity flavor to the smoke. It goes great with the tea. Mohammed and I pass the pipe back and forth.

"That powder you gave me. You said something about time."

He nods.

I feel a bit silly now. The memory of Cassie has faded, and I'm no longer sure it's different from any other memory. Just a tad more real, though, and I know only a few minutes ago, it felt *very* different.

"Did I just go back in time?"

Mohammed stares at me and then just takes another toke of the pipe.

What a lunatic he must think I am. Go back in time? How about using one of the rugs from the carpet schools to fly to Luxor? How about finding a genie in a bottle and having three wishes granted?

I drink my tea, hoping for once that Mohammed didn't understand me. I can't help but stare at him, and I imagine my own face with a pleading look.

He smiles again, not ashamed of his few yellowed teeth. "You go to time? Now?"

Out on the street, there's a clatter of noise as a tour bus pulls up on the other side of the street. Japanese this time. They all pile out and look around in wonder. Tourists only ever stop in this part of town if they have extra time after visiting the quarry and the dam, so they must be a bit ahead of schedule. The tour guides tell them about the surprise shopping trip, and the visitors all thank her and traipse off to various stalls. None will come here, since they're afraid of any place that looks like it sells food or drink. They're hunting for cheap cotton clothes and miniature sphinxes made of fake alabaster.

"Yes. I mean it sounds silly, I know, but I think I was back with my girlfriend."

I rub my hands down my cheeks and close my eyes. *Fuck, what a mess.*

"You see girl?"

"I mean, it was like I was back two years ago. I left your felucca and was back in 1982."

He nods and again takes another sip of his tea.

"You travel your life in order. Why?"

"Why?" I didn't understand and just shook my head.

"Why remember past but not future?"

His question sounded silly. Of course people could remember the past and not the future, because the future hasn't happened yet.

"Past and future same. Like string with bead on it. You move bead from one end to other. Powder is gift of time. Now, you move own bead where you want."

"What? That makes no sense."

"Sorry. English bad."

"No, no. I understood you just fine, but how can somebody move their 'bead' to a place they haven't lived yet?"

"You try. You see."

Hard to argue with that, but neither was I willing to try to jump into a future time. I couldn't figure out how that might work, even theoretically, let alone for real.

I drank the rest of my tea in silence and took one last drag of the pipe before wandering back home and leaving Mohammed to chat with the owner again.

Chapter 4
Anjou (1975)

I'm at home with Mom and Dad. I'm 13.

I got here by thinking about Mom. Today is May 29th—her birthday. I was with Achmed when I just happened to think about her. I guess it was because he was talking to Shani again. It's been a few days since the accident on the boat, and he doesn't need the bandages any more. Shani was washing him off.

He's the same age I am now.

Shani frowned and for some reason that made me think of my own mother, and here I am.

At first I felt really small and skinny, but that passed soon. Now I just feel like me.

"Henry!"

Mom's voice is sharp, and I jump up and run into the house. "Mom?"

I can't help staring at her. She's old. Almost forty. The wrinkles on her face seem to scream her age all around. I wonder where Dad is. He's not in the condo, unless he's sleeping, but that wouldn't be like him.

"I need you to clean up your room."

I nod and start up the stairs.

That's not enough. She calls out, "Why do I have to do everything around here? You'd think I could have one damned day off."

Her voice stops me on my climb, but I don't turn around to look at her. There's no point. I know I'd see anger and bitterness, directed at me because I'm the only person in sight. If Suzie were here, she could just as easily be the one getting blasted. Suzie moved out when she turned eighteen, a few months ago. Lucky her.

I don't have much of an answer for Mom, so I start climbing up the steps again and close the door behind me after I enter my room.

The bed is unmade and there's a glass of water, half-empty on the bedside table. My blue pajamas are on the chair at my desk. I take care of these things, but I don't see anything else. I look critically around the room. All my games are piled neatly on a shelf, my plastic vampire models all in their place, no other dirty clothes scattered anywhere. I'm not sure Mom actually looked in my room to see if it was messy, just assumed it was.

I leave the door closed. Let her think I'm doing lots of clean-up before going downstairs again.

Sitting at my desk, I pick up my O-Pee-Chee hockey cards. The check lists are sitting square in the middle of my desk. Three players are unchecked, and it's driving me crazy. Of course, one of the three is Henri Richard. He's retiring this year, so I *really* need his card.

I hear a crash from downstairs. And another. Some kind of glass thing. Happy Birthday, Mom.

I'm quiet, hoping I don't get dragged into whatever is happening down there. Maybe Dad's back. I can't hear him, but Mom is yelling at someone. Or something. Even though I know she can't hear me, I barely move, not wanting to alert her I'm still here.

After about ten minutes, it gets quiet again. It's 11:00 in the morning.

Another fifteen minutes go by, and I think it's safe to leave.

I climb down the stairs, being careful to stay on the left side of each step. The right side squeaks sometimes. I can hear snores from the living room, which is good. I breathe a bit easier as I reach the bottom of the stairs.

Bits of something blue are on the floor. Farther over, I see a tiny china head. Larger pieces of the figurine are scattered on the floor, into the living room. It's the Virgin Mary statue I'd given Mom earlier today for her birthday. I thought she'd like it. Guess not.

Part of me wonders if I can glue it back together, but that's just silly.

I run out the front door. Never did see Dad.

Chapter 5
Vancouver (2002)

I wake to hear Cassie crying. I roll over immediately and see her clutching the side of our bed in pain.

"Cass, what is it? Bad dream?"

I lean up on one elbow and reach out to hold her. She cries out in pain when I touch her. Fuck. Something's really wrong. I jump out of the bed and flip on the light. In the far side of the room, Jumbles lifts his head and meows.

"Where's it hurt?"

I don't know what to do. She's covered in sweat and tears.

"Cassie, *where's it hurt?*"

"Dad? What's *wrong?*"

Alaine's standing in the doorway. "Go back to bed, son. I need to help Mom right now."

"What's wrong?" He walks in and clutches Cassie's leg, as if he can stop her pain by hugging her ankle. He's now gulping air, feeling her fear.

She glances down at Alaine and tries to calm down, but she

can't. Some kind of pain keeps ripping into her.

"I'm calling an ambulance." There's a phone on our bedside table, and I call 911. After yelling at the operator to get me help, I drop the phone and go back to my wife.

"It's okay. Help is coming."

She whispers, "My neck. My arm." Just those four words take an enormous amount of energy.

I reposition the pillow beneath her head.

"Try to relax, sweetie."

Alaine is trying not to cry. "Watch out the window for me, Bud. Tell me when the ambulance shows up."

He moves to the window, not wanting to take his eyes off his mother.

"So much pain," Cassie says.

"They're almost here. They'll take care of you."

I hold onto her hand with one hand and carefully move her hair out of her eyes with the other. In all the years we've been together, I've never seen her cry until tonight. Not even when she gave birth to Alaine.

Cassie closes her eyes and grits her teeth. She has no strength in her arms. What could it be?

Herniated disk in her neck, of course.

I remember now. The hospital will diagnose it easily tonight.

She opens her eyes, her beautiful, terrified eyes. "Only a little while longer. They'll give you Demerol at the hospital, and the pain will go away."

Cassie blinks, maybe hoping I'm right, but knowing I should be as in the dark about what's happening to her as she is.

"I promise." I hold her cheeks and stare into her eyes. "The pain will go away."

"There it is!" yells Alaine. He runs down the hall to the front door, and I can hear him open it. After a moment, he yells again, "This way. My Mom is hurt."

Two paramedics look at her and ask me what's wrong. "I think it's a herniated disk. In her neck. She's in a lot of pain."

"When did this start?" asks one of them.

"I just woke up about 15 minutes ago, and she was like this."

I want to scream at him to start working on Cassie; it seems like forever before they do anything. Eventually, they gently lift her onto a stretcher. She cries out again in pain. She can no longer even whisper to me, her body shaking as if she were walking naked in the Arctic. I've chewed the inside of my mouth to shreds, feeling so helpless.

They let me and Alaine both ride in the back of the ambulance. Both of us are dressed in pajamas, and neither of us cares. We just want Cassie to get some relief from the awful pain she's in.

The hospital is only ten minutes away. Feels like ten hours. The siren is whirling away, and I know we're going as fast as we can, but I just want to get her there faster. Faster. Faster.

And then I'm in the waiting room with Alaine. I gasp at the newest time jump. A nurse is leading Cassie over to us in a wheelchair. We both run over to meet her.

Cassie tries to smile, but her face muscles aren't working very well. Her eyes bob around, not focusing on us, but she knows we're there.

The nurse says, "She's okay. Just a little woozy. We've given her some Demerol for the pain, and here's a prescription for

Tylenol 3. Follow the dosage instructions, and the pain should be manageable. You'll need to get her to a neurosurgeon as soon as possible."

"How do I find one?"

"Your family doctor will do the referral."

Cassie tries to stand and falls into me. "Home," she says.

I feel a wave of relief, since it's the first painless word she's said to me all night.

There's a taxi stand outside the hospital and we catch the one in front. It seems weird now to be dressed in pajamas, now that the crisis has passed.

Alaine demands to sit beside Cassie, so I help her into the middle of the back seat with us on either side, and we drive home in silence. There's a calmness in the air, as if we're sailing down the Nile . . .

Memories of Achmed and Mohammed flood through me. They've left solid memories, and I'm looking forward to meeting them for the first time whenever I go back to 1984.

I'm no longer bothered by having memories of my future, of living my life in unconnected bits and pieces. That's just the way my life works. The further in the future, the vaguer the memories are, but that's the same as the memories from the past. I don't remember things that happened when I was ten as well as I do those of last year.

Cassie whispers to Alaine. I tense, wondering if she's in pain, but when he giggles at whatever she says, I'm able to relax.

The taxi pulls up to our home on 43rd Avenue. I brought my wallet with me to the hospital, but I have no cash, so I pay the driver with a credit card, adding a five dollar tip. He doesn't offer any thanks.

"I'll help," says Alaine.

We both guide Cassie into the house and up to the bedroom. She falls back asleep shortly after we tuck her in.

Alaine and I sit beside her on the bed. I move some stray hairs from Cassie's face.

"Is Mom gonna die?"

The question shocks me, and I realize Alaine doesn't know what happened. I hug him tightly to me. "Of course not. She's going to have a very sore neck for a couple of months, but she'll be fine." I smile to reassure him.

Alaine is crying silently. His small body is shaking and I feel terrible. I should have told him what was going on sooner.

"It's okay, Bud. Everything's going to be just fine."

He keeps right on crying. Eventually I lift him up and carry him to his own room. I lay down beside him, cradle him, stroke his head, and kiss his cheek while he falls asleep.

Chapter 6
Vancouver (2012)

I'm fifty years old now, and I feel every sore muscle and extra pound I'm carrying. I don't like myself this way. At least that's what I think now, but it's clear I've never done anything to be in better shape, even though I'll know my future state when I go through the earlier days of my life.

It was hard to get here. I'm near the Gray Zone.

Thinking of my future now, even this close, my memories are clear enough for the next year or so, but after that, it's like they fall into a fog. Every time I try to pierce the haze I get a headache and no answers.

I have a feeling I die then.

This is as close as I've ever gotten, and it was a chore to push myself to 2012. It's easier living any earlier portion of my life, easiest by far to live as a child or young adult. Each year closer to the Gray Zone is slightly harder to reach.

Maybe I shouldn't even try, but there's a part of me that demands to know. *What happens?*

"Henry?"

I must look like an idiot, just staring blankly into space.

"Yeah, I'm going."

"You okay?" Joey blinks and rearranges his thick eyeglasses.

I glance at my watch. Two minutes late already. "Shit. I lost track of time."

The lecture room is just down the hall from my office, so it doesn't take me long. There's thirty-three students in theory, but in practice only about two dozen attend my lectures. Most of the rest dropped off when we started covering quantum mechanics.

"Sorry I'm late, everyone." It's a second year astronomy course, but all the students still look like little kids to me. None of them used the time waiting for me to study. Instead, they've been chatting each other up, sending text messages, or God knows what else with their little thumb pads.

"Today, we'll be continuing our discussion on the nuclear reactions inside a supernova, from a quantum perspective."

Most of the students' eyes migrate to look at me while I write out a couple of basic formulae on the white board.

But after I scribble the first equation, I find I don't much care about the topic. It's all so damned esoteric and specialized. Who cares

(about the Gray Zone)

what the exact sequence of neutrino transformation is? Why worry about the polarization states of gluons? Other people have already wasted years working this stuff out, and if any of my students care, they can just google the answers.

I turn back to the kids. They sit and stare at me like sheep. "Why did God create us?" I ask.

Silence and confusion fills the room for a moment. Finally,

Shelby calls out from the back of the room. "Are you mixing up your classes, Professor?"

A few students chuckle, but they see I'm not laughing.

"No, I'm asking from a scientific perspective, not a theological one. We've talked about all the equations before." I wave at the half-finished ones behind me. "We know they work, but why *should* they? Why would God decide e should be equal to mc^2? Why not mc^3? Why not something totally different altogether?"

Nobody seemed interested in replying.

"Why should the force of gravity be 9.8 meters per second squared?"

I hesitate but then ask, "Why should we be able to remember the past but not the future? All our scientific equations work in either direction. $mc^2 = e$ is just as valid as $e = mc^2$. There's no reason for time to flow forward."

I see Joey sneak in to the back of the class. Even though he's a grad student, he tries to attend as many of my lectures as possible, since he teaches my labs.

Lynda finally answers. "If we could remember the future, we'd be breaking causality, which is a basic feature of our universe." She folds her hands together, unsure if she's right.

"No, that's not it." I turn to my left and Steven adds, "There's no law against causality. It's just never been seen to be broken."

"Quantum computers break it," I say.

"Only by reaching into parallel universes."

"And so, why can't we do the same?"

Steven shrugged and looks at his watch. "Are we going to be getting back to an actual science lecture today? Finals are in three weeks."

Fucker.

He looks at me in defiance, the smartest kid in the class, but he's only interested in the numbers. Equations, variables, reactions, solid answers to clear questions. I could see him working at Mount Palomar one day, but not Cambridge.

I glance around the room and see nobody else is interested in time's arrow, either. I turn and reluctantly finish scribbling the equations I'd started.

God, I feel old.

After finishing the lecture, I cancel the afternoon session. Mornings I teach astronomy, afternoons I teach theology. Day in, day out.

I just can't get the interest up today. Somehow, lecturing on the origin of the universe is more interesting in a science setting, but the students don't give a shit. In theology, the students listen, but only seem to be interested in a single answer.

None of them care about time's arrow.

I leave the UBC campus and drive to our home in Kerrisdale. The nice neighborhood seems like window dressing draped over my psyche.

"Hey, you're home early."

Cassie gives me a welcome hug. I don't want to let her go—like I'd slump to the floor in this saggy old body if she didn't support me. I pull her head to my shoulder and wish I'd taken her to Egypt all those years ago. She kept saying she wanted to go, to see if we could track down Achmed and maybe even Mohammed, see what happened to them, but . . .

"You okay?"

"Yeah. It's just . . ."

"Henry?"

I shuffle into the living room and sit on the couch. "I always wanted to be called Henri."

"Henri?"

"Like the Pocket Rocket."

She stares at me without understanding. Who can blame her? I must look and sound like an idiot. She clutches at my hand.

"Can I get you a beer? Something?"

I close my eyes and shake my head. "Just tired."

I can feel her fingers rubbing my hand. Nobody ever was as lucky as me in marriage. "I wish I knew what happened to Achmed."

"Alaine's over at a friend's house. Why don't we go out for a nice dinner at the Keg?"

I take a deep breath and blink my eyes open. She has a tissue ready, and I use it to wipe my face. I nod. "That'd be nice."

"Maybe you should have a quick shower first."

I blow my nose into the tissue and walk up the stairs. *Old* creaks through my knees. I wish I was young.

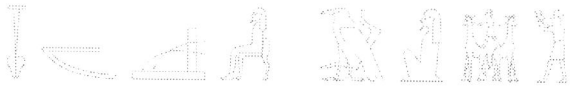

Chapter 7
Anjou (1975)

And then I am.

As I walk up the front walk to my house, a weird feeling flushes through me. I shake it off. I've long since realized there's no point in trying to concentrate on what's about to happen; even if I can locate the memory, it doesn't change anything.

I'm thirteen, and I feel about a jillion times better than I did just a few moments ago. The heavy weight is gone, the sadness evaporated. Instead, summer sunshine hugs me like a duvet, and I know I'm grinning from ear to ear.

Ten minutes ago, we left school. *We*, as in me and Amy. I walked her home, and before she ducked inside her basement apartment, she giggled, looked around, and kissed me. On the lips!

That's the memory I want right now, not some weird thing that happens way in the future when I'll be a thousand years old or whatever.

Amy Sterling kissed me!

"Suzie!" I couldn't wait to tell my sister; her car was in the driveway. She's always teasing me about how much I like Amy.

Three-thirty on a Wednesday afternoon. That's about the only time it's safe to yell in the house. Mom works Monday, Wednesday, and Friday afternoons down at Place Ville Marie, helping sell clothes or something.

"Suzie!"

I run to the back of the house, but nothing. Cigarette smoke hangs in the air, as always, and there's two empty cans of beer on the sink. Dad must have come home for lunch.

The TV is on, tuned to *The Match Game*. After clicking it off, I call out one more time. Finally I hear—

(something terrible)

—a sound from upstairs. I'm not sure what it is. For another few moments, the house is silent again, but I can feel my heart pounding.

I climb the stairs, not worrying about the creaks. When I'm halfway up, Suzie's cries become more clear, and I run the rest of the way up. I want to hurry, but at the same time I don't want to go to her at all. It's not good. I'm sweating and biting my lip. Forcing my feet forward like I'm walking through quicksand, the bathroom door calls to me like a siren.

This time I'm whispering. "Suzie?"

She continues crying. I can see her legs on the bathroom floor, the door hiding the rest of her. She's wearing the long white socks that are her trademark.

"Mom . . ." she cries.

I finally reach the bathroom and push the door open with a shaking hand. The door bangs against the tub.

I'm frozen with fear. Mom is covered with blood, dried and sticky. I think there must have been water in the tub earlier, but it's all gone now, and a pink wash covers the porcelain. Her hair is matted, and long cuts cover her arms from her elbows to her wrists.

I've never seen her naked before.

Her head slumps to the side, as if she's licking the tub.

Part of me refuses to believe what I see. I reach down and shake her, then gasp at the sticky blood covering my own hand.

I realize my pants are wet. I've peed myself.

"Mom?"

I finally break off and look at Suzie, who's head is down. She's still sobbing but no longer making any noise. Her hair covers her face, but I push it all back and hold her to me. *Somehow, I have to be strong*, I know. I have to help my sister.

But I have no idea how.

She looks up, and her face is all red. I almost don't recognize her.

"We have to call for help," I say. "Maybe they can save her."

Suzie starts laughing. "Help her? Are you stupid? She's fucking dead!"

"But . . ."

I stare back at Mom, watch the blood congeal between her legs, see her sagging breasts with their awful gray color.

And I know Suzie's right, of course. There's nothing anyone can do.

I start to cry.

Chapter 8
Montreal (1982)

Cassie and I met a month ago. That's a month ago as the calendar turns, not a month ago in my own memory. My heart knows I'm falling madly in love with her for the first time.

"Where to now?" she asks.

When I wrap my arms around her and pull her close to kiss her, I'm lost. Cassie is my whole universe, and all I want to do is hold her.

Eventually, we separate and I lick my lips. This is the happiest time of my life.

A nagging *something* pokes at me, reminding me of just having left Mom's body, but in my new time reference, that happened a long time ago. Seven years ago, not the seven minutes ago I know it really was.

"Back down?"

Cassie nods. We've spent the afternoon at Beaver Lake, on the top of Mount Royal. We grab a couple cans of Coke at the chalet overlooking Montreal and start walking down the makeshift steps and pathways that lead us eventually to downtown.

We don't really need to talk about where we'll go from there. I just take the lead, and we head to my apartment in the McGill student ghetto.

Our first time.

She knows where we're going, since I've told her where I live, but she smiles and laughs and we both know it's right.

Since the parade, we've grown closer and closer. When my eyes shut each night, I visualize her lying beside me, my fingers running through her long red hair, her blue eyes staring into mine. I can see her perfect body in my mind anytime I want. It's like a photograph of her is tattooed on my retina.

And I know she feels the same about me. She shows it in every move, every kiss, every caress.

We get to my apartment after about an hour's walk down the mountain and through the city. The ghetto is full of cheap, unspectacular housing for McGill students, as well as low-income people who just can't afford anything better. It's not a place most people are proud of living in, but it's mine.

I lead Cassie up the three flights of stairs to my room. Clean and neat. Has been since I met her; I knew one day she'd be seeing it.

Cassie's home is in Westmount, where all the rich English people live. Her dad's a lawyer when he's not banging the drum for the marching accordion band.

"Nice."

I smile, knowing she's being kind. "Not quite what you're used to."

"It's *nice*," she says again. "Show me around."

I can't help but laugh. "It's pretty much what you see here. That's where I do my homework." I point to a small desk piled with astronomy and religious texts. "That's where I cook. The bathroom is right there, and my bedroom is over here."

She walks over to the small kitchenette and then flips through the textbooks.

"No TV?"

I shake my head. "I have a radio."

She clicks the radio on. I normally listen to a local rock station, and *Bohemian Rhapsody* by Queen drifts out from the tiny speakers.

"Show me the bedroom."

My mouth suddenly goes dry. I nod and take her hand, as I open the bedroom door. There's only a small single bed and a dresser in the corner. Thank God I'd remembered to hide all my dirty laundry before I left this morning.

Cassie kisses me and after a moment, we lie down in the bed. In a few moments, all my dreams come true.

Chapter 9
Vancouver (2014)

There's somebody in the house.

I've snapped awake and am lying quietly beside Cassie. She hasn't awoken. I don't move, not wanting the swish of the sheets to drown out the sound.

I know I heard something. It wasn't a dream.

But now the house is silent. The only sound I can hear is the almost nonexistent traffic noise filtering in from the other side of the house. There's no creaks, no whispers from downstairs, but I know I heard something.

They must have cut the alarm system.

I think of waking Cassie, but I'm not sure she'd believe me.

There's a baseball bat leaning against my side table. I grip it tightly, careful not to pull it too fast and bang it against the table. The bat's never been used; it's been waiting for—

(the Gray Zone)

—for today.

I look around and try my hardest to remember what's about

to happen. Nothing. No memory at all. It's true: I'm in the Gray Zone. I have no sense at all about what's going to happen. For the longest time, I've had an internal safety net, but not now.

My breathing is rushed, and I have trouble convincing my feet to move forward. I glance behind me to be sure Cassie is still asleep. It's not too late to change my mind and wake her. . .

I inch out to the hallway. I still haven't heard anything, but I can *feel* someone downstairs. I'm holding the bat in both hands over my shoulder. I take a deep breath and remember the plan for intruders. Don't strangle the bat. Hold it firm but not *too* tight. I'm the only person I know who keeps a weapon ready. I knew I'd need it one day.

As I creep down the stairs, I question myself. Should I turn the lights on? Doing that would warn the burglar. If he's armed, I'd be a sitting duck.

Alaine is visiting my sister in Montreal. I'm glad he's not here for this, but I wish I wasn't the only one creeping down the stairs.

And then, I hear it again. A shuffling sound, like someone pushing furniture or sliding some of our belongings off shelves.

My head is spinning, and my knees almost give out. Panic sets in. I take a deep breath and move to the kitchen, where the sound is coming from.

I silently offer a prayer to a God I'm not sure I believe in.

The kitchen is pitch black. The windows face Montgomery Park, and there's no light at all from there.

I'm holding the bat close to my side, aimed straight ahead.

Shush.

The scraping sound is too much for me, and I lose control of myself. The shape is coming toward me, and I smash the bat

down over and over. There's a deep thud at first, followed by the sound of bone cracking. My hands are wet but I keep hitting and hitting. A groan. More hits and more blood.

And then sweet quietness.

"Oh my God," I cry. I stumble backward, banging into the door jamb.

Cassie calls out from our bedroom. "Henry! What happened?"

I'm too scared to yell at her to call the police.

She rushes down the stairs, carrying a candle, which hurts my eyes.

"My God, Henry, what . . . ?"

We both stare at the prone body. At first the head is just a bloody pulp, raw hamburger. Through the mess, though, I begin to recognize Alaine's motionless body.

It's been three days since we buried our son, and I still feel like I'm walking through a fog all the time. I force myself every day to climb out of bed, push myself to face the world. Most particularly, to face Cassie.

She sleeps in Alaine's bed each night. That first day, after the police left, I tried to hold her, but she just stood stiff as a board.

"I need to digest everything," she said as she slipped out of my grasp.

I know she's trying to figure out how everything could have happened. How was it Alaine decided to come home early and surprise us? How could the power fail the same damned night he arrived home? How could I have panicked and . . .

Over and over, I replay that night in my mind. I've seen it

a thousand times now. The shadow moving toward me in the darkness, my fear overtaking me, my hand gripping the handle.

My son dead.

This morning, I've spent hours on the couch, doing nothing but stare into space and remember Alaine. I remember the first time we went salmon fishing, and when I first took him skiing at Whistler. The cheering when we sat in row six at the men's hockey final at the 2010 Olympics. And the times when he was small, when he would sit and fall asleep on my lap while I whispered bedtime stories in his ear.

I wish I knew what memories Cassie was reliving, but she avoids me. Since the cremation, she hasn't talked to me at all. She sometimes leaves the house for hours at a time, but I don't know where she goes.

The grandfather clock strikes noon. I can't believe it's that late already. I'm sure I only sat down a while ago, but it's been almost six hours.

Cassie hasn't come down for breakfast yet. I walk to Alaine's room, wondering if I should wake her. I silently open the door, but she's not there.

I can hear the small shower in Alaine's ensuite bathroom.

The room is full of memories, and I haven't come in here since his death. There's a stack of old CDs sitting beside his portable stereo, a few paperback books in a clumsy pile, and clothes scattered on the chair. Cassie hasn't touched them.

A trickle of water runs out from under the bathroom door. At first I don't understand and stare at it from the fog of my deadened mind.

(Karma Chameleon . . .)

"Cassie?" No answer. I yell again, "Cassie!" as I push open the door. Water rushes out and I see her slumped in the corner of the shower stall, red-faced and covered in running blood. The razor blades are still in her limp fingers.

Her eyes gaze out to me, but they see nothing. I don't know how long she's been here, but it's too late for me to do anything.

"No!" I cry. "Cassie, no!"

I try to focus. Turn off the water. Check to see if she's breathing or has a pulse. I pull her up and carry her to Alaine's bed, rubbing all the blood off with the blankets and sheets.

She stares up at the ceiling.

Her limbs are stiff, and one arm points to the ceiling from the elbow up.

I jump in time for a second and see the dead face of my mother accusing me. Then I'm back with Cassie.

"My love," I whisper. "I'm so sorry."

I crawl into the bed beside her and cry. I can barely breathe with the wracking of my body. I've killed her just as surely as I killed Alaine, and I'm overwhelmed with grief and guilt.

I kiss her cold cheek and pull her to me. I can't leave her. She and Alaine are everything to me. How can they both be gone?

The pain is too much. I reach out in my mind to find another time to be. Any other time.

Chapter 10
Vancouver (2010)

I'm sitting with Cassie, each of us holding a glass of Merlot, watching an old movie on TV. The love seat we share is perfect for us; I can feel her hip on mine, and I'm sure that half the time we watch the movie, my hand is resting on her thigh.

Weird. I don't know when I came from. I almost always know when I've just been. I yawn, trying to stay awake.

Alaine is sleeping on the floor, a small pillow the only hint of comfort he was interested in. He always likes watching a movie with us on Friday nights, but I know that won't always be true. For now, I'm blessed.

"Pretty boring, isn't it?" Cassie yawns and plops her head on my shoulder. "I'm not surprised he didn't make it till the end."

"Can't win them all."

I pour a bit more wine for both of us as the closing credits roll.

"Want to watch the news?"

She shrugs. "Suppose."

I flip the channel, and we wait for the commercials to end. And then the lights go out.

Cassie snaps her head off my shoulder. "Damn, not again."

I carefully walk over to the mantel and light a candle. "It's okay. We're prepared this time."

She looks beautiful in the glow of the candle. Rather than go flip the circuit breaker, I sit back on the couch and kiss her.

She holds me close and sighs.

"You're beautiful."

Cassie smiles. "Go fix the power, please."

"Don't you think this is romantic?"

She laughs. "We're too old for romance. I'm happy with getting to sleep by ten o'clock these days."

I light a second candle and leave it on the coffee table for her while I walk to the stairs leading to the basement.

"I really think we should get an electrician in," she calls over the railing. I wince, knowing I've promised to get the wiring redone for years. Somehow it never seems important. It's only a quick trip down to the basement to flip the breaker back on. What harm can a few seconds of darkness do?

So much for romance.

Right now, I just feel rejected. When the lights are back, I blow out the candle. Upstairs, I hear Cassie waking Alaine and sending him to bed. She clicks the TV off.

Sometimes, I wish she'd enjoy the occasional blackout. It really does put her in a wonderful light.

As much as I wish they didn't, her words hurt. *I'm happy with getting to sleep by ten o'clock these days.* I know she didn't mean to slap at me, but it's hard to avoid the inference. Forty-eight years old. It's not like we're ancient or anything. Alaine's only fourteen. Cassie and I have a long time to grow old together, but

I dread the day Alaine moves out. We probably only have him living with us another six or eight years. Then our little family unit will be very different.

For once, I try hard to look into my future memories. I know we'll have many wonderful times to come, but then I hit the wall. That Gray Zone in 2014, only four years from now. I see nothing after it starts. Just a fog enveloping my life.

I sometimes wonder if I can avoid ever going into there, but it seems unlikely. I'm going to live that long, I know, so surely I have to experience whatever it is that happens then. Don't I?

Meanwhile, I grab onto the memory of taking Alaine to Jericho Beach next month. He'll love that trip. We'll walk out into English Bay, feel the cool water splash up on us both, cook hot dogs in a sand pit, and watch the sun set over the water. Boy's day. I can't wait for that.

Chapter 11
Anjou (1975)

"Shit. She hitting the bottle again?"

"Yeah."

"Happy fucking birthday, Mom."

Suzie stands aside and lets me into her apartment. I wish I could give her a hug, but it's a bit awkward now that she's already started dissing Mom.

"You want a Coke?"

I shrug. "Sure."

I've only been to Suzie's place a couple of other times and never really clued in till now that I only go to visit when Mom's had a hard day.

The apartment is awful. It's so small it feels like the walls are going to fall in on me. It stinks of cigarettes. Suzie lights one and then hunts through the small fridge to find a pop.

"Guess I don't have any. I got beer." She laughs but opens a can anyhow.

"S'okay. I'm not really thirsty."

She takes a long drink of the beer, looks like half the can. Like mother like daughter, I guess.

There's a long silence in the room. With Suzie being five years older than me, it's a big gulf. Sometimes it seems like she's more an aunt than a sister, but then I remember when I was little, she'd play cards with me. She taught me *Go Fish* and *War*. I know in the future we grow closer as the age difference becomes less important. Her second husband will be a close friend of mine.

"Wanna watch TV? I think there's some—" She hunts for the TV Guide, but I don't really care what she thinks is on.

"I think we should do something," I say. "About Mom, I mean."

The idea seems to bounce off her and fall flat on the floor. She doesn't say anything for a minute, just blows a smoke ring and takes another drink of her beer.

"What do you mean?" she finally asks.

I know I could focus on the memory if I want, but it's too big, too scary. I close my mind off to any specifics.

"Something's gonna happen to her."

Suzie shakes her head. "Nothing's going to *happen*. Jesus. She's just going to grow into a miserable old cow, like she's been doing. What happened today?"

I remember the figurine I'd gotten Mom and how it lay shattered on the floor. For some reason I'm ashamed to tell Suzie about it. Afraid she'll think I'm an idiot or something for even buying Mom a gift.

"Just a lot of yelling."

"Yeah." She sits in the wooden chair beside me. "It's okay. You can stay here as long as you want."

"But she's—"

A quick flash shows me Mom's body in the bathtub, swimming in red. Now it's gone, as if it were never really there.

"Henry? What's wrong?"

In my mind, I hear Boy George and Culture Club singing "Karma Chameleon." Is that song even out yet? I don't know.

"Henry?"

I shake my head. "I . . . I don't know. Something."

And a horrible thought. What if it's a better future without Mom?

I close my eyes and push the thought away. It's not too late. I can help Mom. Stop her from . . .

Karma's a bitch.

Was that part of the song? I can't remember.

Suzie stands. "You want a beer? Mom'd kill me but maybe it'd be good for you."

Without waiting for an answer, she grabs two cans from the fridge, pops the top on them both and puts one in front of me. She's right—Mom would *definitely* kill her for that. I can almost hear the seconds ticking away as I stare at the beer. Finally I grab it. It tastes awful.

"Happy Birthday," I whisper.

Chapter 12
Vancouver (2014)

There's somebody in the house.

What the hell? I'm careful not to wake Cassie as I move to the bedroom doorway. Almost as an afterthought, I pick the baseball bat from beside the bedside table.

Downstairs is silent now, but I know I heard something. *Someone.*

My mouth is dry, and my chest is heaving from fear. I take long deep breaths, gathering the courage to act. I glance back; I haven't woken Cassie. I almost wonder if part of me wants her to wake, so I don't have to face the intruder alone.

Of course not.

The stairs are quiet beneath my feet. I think of turning the lights on, but that would just give the intruder an advantage.

I'm more frightened than I've ever been. I *know* somebody is down there, and he's not going to be—

Jesus.

—it's just hit me. I'm in the Gray Zone.

The Gray Zone

I've never been in the Gray Zone before. I stop at the landing halfway down the stairs. Does this mean I'm going to die here?

My hand is like a vice on the baseball bat, and I loosen my grip a bit. I need to think straight, not panic.

There's still no noise, but I know what I heard, and I know there's someone down there.

I maneuver to the kitchen and slowly push the door open.

At first, nothing. But, then, a shadow moves and is coming toward me. He's attacking. *Fuck!* I hit without thinking, the force of the crunch pushing my arm back. "Oh, my God," I cry.

Hit, hit, hit.

The man falls to the floor, and for a moment, all I can see is a slightly darker shadow.

"Henry! What happened?"

I can't answer Cassie. My words are gone.

She rushes down beside me and flicks the light switch. Nothing.

"Stay back. I don't know if—"

"What happened?"

"I think . . . I think he's dead."

"Oh, my God."

Cassie moves to the mantel and lights a candle. She walks slowly back toward me. I keep the bat aimed at the body.

And then the light shows my son, and my world falls apart.

𓀀 𓀁 𓀂

In the days that follow, I walk around in a daze, and only barely stop myself from drinking all day and all night. There are arrangements to make, and the police are investigating the death.

Cassie shuns me, and I understand. She needs time to get over it. She needs time to forgive me. I need time to forgive myself. She's sleeping in Alaine's room.

Today, I woke and couldn't find her. I walk up to check on her and find the bed empty, the shower running. For a moment, I relax, but then I notice the water running out from under the shower stall.

Chapter 13
Vancouver (2014)

Oh my God, I think I'm in the Gray Zone.

I've never been here before. My whole life has been an open book to me until now. I have no memory of anything that happens in the Gray Zone and have always been afraid of it. Somehow I'm here.

A rush of déjà vu runs though me, and then it's gone.

Shit. I don't want to be here.

I can't even wish my way out, back to my "normal" life.

It's dark. And silent.

Cassie's asleep, but—my senses come to attention. *Oh, my God, there's somebody downstairs.*

I'm holding my breath, listening . . .

. . . "Fuck, fuck, fuck! No. Cassie!"

But I know it's too late. Her eyes are glazed over, and there's no life left in her.

    She's covered in dried blood, but I can't help myself. I climb into the tub and pull her to me. "Cassie, my love. Don't leave me."

    She doesn't answer. My tears wash some of the blood off one cheek, but she doesn't move or answer me. I know she can't, but I want her to anyway.

    I collapse into her and cry for what seems like forever.

Chapter 14
Aswan (1984)

I climb off the cruise ship after it docks at Aswan and stare at the city. It's beautiful. Somehow there's an immediate sense of peace and goodwill. I'm not sure how to explain it. The feeling just permeates everything.

The air is clean and smells of seafood. I have no plan of where to go. I vaguely remember I'll be spending several months here, so I know I'll like it.

Even after all these—

(decades)

—years, it's still a bit weird to know I can remember my future any time I want. Well, except for the Gray Zone—I've never been there. One day . . .

Local men shout out to the tourists walking off the ship, offering to take them to the best markets or the quarry or help them find a felucca. Of course, most of the tourists are in groups, and the tour guides ignore all the locals, leading the visitors down the edge of the river to wherever they're going.

My time here is less planned. I just hopped onto the boat from Luxor. I'm not good as part of a group. Would rather explore on my own.

A cab driver is waving and smiling at me. "American?" It's always the first question.

"Canadian."

"Ah, Canada Dry!" He laughs at the same joke I've heard a hundred times since arriving in Cairo two weeks ago.

What the heck.

"Can you take me to the Aswan Dam?"

"Ah. Of course, sir. Only five hundred Egyptian Pounds."

"No. One hundred."

"Sir, is a long way. A very long way."

We eventually agree on two hundred pounds, and I climb into the back of the tiny cab. It stinks of cigarettes.

The ride is pleasant, and I take mental notes of some parts of town I want to come back to. The drive takes about a half hour, and I pay the driver, who immediately starts looking for someone to take back to town. "Allah bless you, sir," he says. I wave good-bye.

The dam is huge. Standing at one end, I can barely see the other end.

"Baksheesh?"

I turn to see a young boy standing beside me. He can't be more than twelve years old, but ages are hard to determine in Egypt.

"No."

I almost walk away, when he says, "Thank you, sir." When he bows, I feel a rush of recognition from long ago.

"You speak English."

"Some. No good like you, sir."

His curly black hair shines in the sunlight, but it's his smile that really captures me. Hypnotizing.

"My name Achmed, sir."

One day I'd like to have a son.

Afterword

Where do story ideas come from? *The Gray Zone* is partly set in Aswan, Egypt. Although Egypt is a poor country compared to the U.S. or other western countries, it's one of the most fascinating places I've ever visited. In particular, Aswan is amazing. The people there are some of the friendliest you could ever hope to find.

I've been to Aswan several times and it's one of the few places I could imagine myself living outside of North America. I hope you have a chance to visit there one day.

The rest of the story is set in both Vancouver and Montreal, two cities I've lived in for long periods of time. They're both wonderful cities. I've wanted to set a story in these three places for some time.

Of course *The Gray Zone* is not a travel book. It's a book about characters. Hopefully characters you learned to care about.

The idea for the story came to me in the middle of the night. For some reason I remembered Stephen Hawking's comment in his book *A Brief History of Time*, wondering why we couldn't remember the future as easily as the past. I asked myself what life would be like for somebody who actually could do that. And then I added the twist that he could live his life in any sequence he liked, and I had the basic premise of the story.

But a premise is not a story. The story is what happens to Henry as he lives his fractured life with the woman of his dreams, and losing her due to his own actions. It's a story of happiness and sorrow. I hope you felt some of that as you read it.

Thanks to all my readers for picking up this book. If you wish, drop me a line at john@johnrlittle.com and let me know what you thought.

About the Author

John R. Little is the Bram Stoker Award-wining author of *Miranda, Placeholders, Dreams in Black and White,* and *The Memory Tree*.

He has been writing horror and dark fantasy stories since his first publications in *The Twilight Zone, Weird Tales,* and other magazines in the early 1980s. He's been published in many other magazines since, including *Cavalier, Dark Discoveries,* and *Doorways*.

Many of his stories have appeared in anthologies including *Shivers IV, 100 Great Fantasy Short Short Stories,* and others. His work has been translated into German, Italian, French, and Spanish. Upcoming will be stories in *Dark Delicacies 3* and *Legends of the Mountain State 3*.

The Memory Tree was John's first novel, and he's honored that it was nominated for the Bram Stoker Award. His novella, *Place-*

holders, was nominated for the Black Quill award.

Miranda (also published by Bad Moon Books) won both the Black Quill and Stoker. Bad Moon will be publishing a collection of John's short stories in 2010 called *Little Things*.

John lives in the most beautiful place in the world, a suburb of Vancouver, Canada, surrounded by snow-capped mountains on one side and tall evergreen trees on the other. He is currently working on his next novel.